W9-DIS-382

CAPTAIN UNDERPANTS AND THE PERILOUS PLOT OF PROFESSOR POOPYPANTS

CAPTAIN UNDERPANTS
AND THE PERILOUS PLOT OF PROFESSOR POOPYPANTS
The Fourth Epic Novel by
DAV PILKEY
GIDGET HAMSTERBRAINS
SCHOLASTIC INC.

Published by Scholastic Inc., *Publishers since 1920.*
SCHOLASTIC and associated logos are trademarks
and/or registered trademarks of Scholastic Inc.
CAPTAIN UNDERPANTS and related designs are trademarks
and/or registered trademarks of Dav Pilkey.

Library of Congress Control Number: 99-054825

ISBN 978-0-439-04997-9

31 30 29 28 17 18 19/0

Printed in the U.S.A. 23
First printing, February 2000

Book design by Dav Pilkey and Kathleen Westray

CHAPTERS

In our last three adventures, we tried to save our crazy principal from disaster. He thought he was a real superhero— but he wasn't!
We didn't think things could get any worse— but they did!

THE TOP-SECRET TRUTH ABOUT CAPTAIN UNDERPANTS
ALL New
Once upon A time There Were Two Cool Kids Named George and HArold.
We Are Awe-Some
Me Too.
They had a mean old Principle named MR. Krupp.
Blah Blah Blah!
Mr. Krupp was very mean to George and Harold.
Blah Blah Blah
So They Bought The 3-D Hypno Ring.
They Used it To Hypnotise Mr. Krupp.
You wiLL OBEY US
Okey Dokey

They had a Lot of advenchers. One Time they even got ATTACKED By A U.F.O.!!!

UH, OH!

The only way George And Harold can Stop Captain Underpants From causing troubel is by Poring water on His head...

TreeHousE Comix
INC.

CHAPTER 1

GEORGE AND HAROLD

This is George Beard and Harold Hutchins. George is the kid on the left with the tie and the flat-top. Harold is the one on the right with the T-shirt and the bad haircut. Remember that now.

All of the “experts” at Jerome Horwitz Elementary School had their opinions about George and Harold. Their guidance counselor, Mr. Rected, thought the boys suffered from A.D.D. The school psychologist, Miss Labler, diagnosed them with A.D.H.D. And their mean old principal, Mr. Krupp, thought they were just plain old ***B.A.D.***!

But if you ask me, George and Harold simply suffered from I.B.S.S. (Incredibly Boring School Syndrome).

You see, George and Harold weren't really bad kids. They were actually very bright, good-natured boys. Their only problem was that they were bored in school. So they took it upon themselves to "liven things up" for everybody. Wasn't that thoughtful of them?

Unfortunately, George and Harold's *thoughtfulness* got them into trouble every now and then. Sometimes it got them into a *LOT* of trouble. And one time it got them into *so much* trouble, it almost caused the entire planet to be taken over by a ruthless, maniacal, mad-scientist guy in a giant robot suit!

But before I can tell you that story, I have to tell you *this* story. . . .

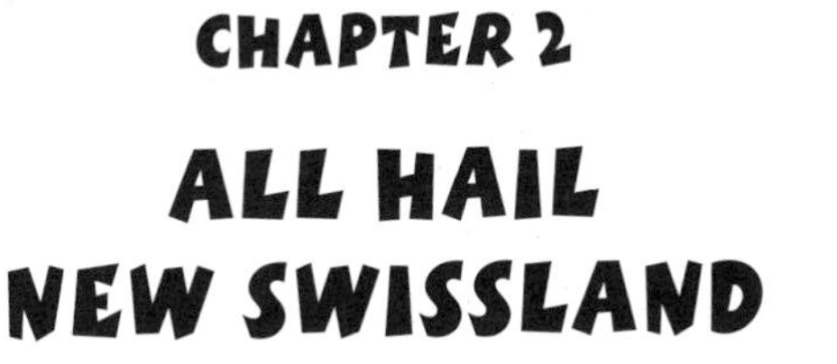

CHAPTER 2
ALL HAIL NEW SWISSLAND

As everybody knows, New Swissland is a small country just southeast of Greenland. You probably know all about New Swissland's natural resources and systems of government. But here's something about New Swissland that I'll bet you didn't know: Everybody in New Swissland has a silly name.

Just ask their president, the Honorable Chuckles Jingleberry McMonkeyburger Jr. or his lovely wife, Stinky.

They'll tell you all about New Swissland's proud "silly name" heritage. They'll tell you about the cultural significance of silly names. And then they'll probably tell you a really, really long boring story of how this stupid tradition got started. We'll skip that part, OK?

Just remember that everybody in New Swissland has a silly name. From the richest to the poorest, from the dumbest to the smartest.

And speaking of the *smartest*, let me introduce you to Professor Pippy P. Poopypants. That's a statue of him down there in the bottom right-hand corner of the page. Now Pippy P. Poopypants was probably the smartest person in all of New Swissland. He graduated at the head of his class at Chunky Q. Boogernose University, and afterward spent all of his time creating wild and fantastic inventions.

Let's look in on him, shall we?

Back in his private laboratory, Professor Pippy P. Poopypants was just putting the finishing touches on two wonderful new inventions: the Shrinky-Pig 2000, and the Goosy-Grow 4000.

Professor Poopypants called for his assistant, Porkbelly Funkyskunk. "Mr. Funkyskunk," Pippy yelled, "I am now ready to test my new inventions!"

Porkbelly took notes while the professor aimed his Shrinky-Pig 2000 at a hideous pile of trash.

"BLLLLLLZZZZRRRRK!"

A powerful beam of energy blasted the garbage heap. Suddenly, the large pile of trash shrank to the size of a gumball.

"Hooray! It works!" cried Professor Poopypants. "Now I must try the Goosy-Grow 4000."

Pippy and Porkbelly aimed the Goosy-Grow 4000 at an ordinary hot dog with mustard.

“GGGGLLUUZZZZZZZZRRRRRT!” went another bright beam of energy.

Suddenly, the hot dog grew and grew until it crashed through the walls of the laboratory.

"We did it!" exclaimed Porkbelly.

"What do you mean, *WE*?!!?" yelled Professor Poopypants. "*I* did it! *I'm* the GENIUS! You're just a lowly assistant—and don't you forget it!"

"Sorry, boss," said Porkbelly.

"With these two inventions," exclaimed Professor Poopypants, "I will be able to solve the world's garbage problem AND create enough food for everyone on the entire planet!"

Finally, it looked as if all of the Earth's dilemmas would be fixed forever. But who would have believed that in just a few short weeks, Professor Poopypants would be trying to take over the planet in a fit of frenzied rage?

Well, dear readers, the tragic tale is about to unfold. But before I can tell you that story, I have to tell you *this* story.

CHAPTER 3

THE FIELD TRIP

Jerome Horwitz Elementary School was having its big annual field trip to Piqua Pizza Palace. All of the kids had brought their permission slips and were lined up to get on the bus. George and Harold could hardly wait to eat pizza and play video games all afternoon.

"This is gonna RULE!" said George.

"Yeah, if we ever get there," said Harold.

"Hey," said George, "let's change the letters around on the school sign while we're waiting."

"Good idea," said Harold.

So George and Harold ran over to the sign and began their, um, *thoughtfulness*. Unfortunately, the boys didn't notice a dark, foreboding presence lurking nearby in the bushes.

"A-HA!" cried Mr. Krupp. "I caught you boys *red-handed*!"

"Uh-oh!" said George.

"Heh-heh," laughed Harold. "Th-this is just a little joke."

"A *JOKE*?!!?" yelled Mr. Krupp. "Do you boys think that's funny???"

George and Harold thought for a moment. "Well . . . *yeah*," said George.

"Don't *you*?" asked Harold.

"*NO*, I don't think it's funny!" yelled Mr. Krupp. "I think it's rude and offensive!"

"That's why it's funny," said George.

"Oh," said Mr. Krupp. "You boys like to laugh, huh? Well, here's a good one: You two are officially *BANNED* from the school field trip! Instead of eating pizza, you'll spend the afternoon cleaning up the teachers' lounge! Isn't *that* funny?!!?"

"No way!" said Harold.

"That's not funny at all," said George. "That's cruel and unusual punishment."

"That's why it's funny!" Mr. Krupp snarled.

CHAPTER 4

LEFT BEHIND

Mr. Krupp marched George and Harold over to the janitor's closet.

"You can use these supplies to clean the teachers' lounge," said Mr. Krupp. "I want it SPOTLESS by the time we get back!"

Mr. Krupp went back outside, climbed onto the school bus, and laughed loudly as the buses pulled away. The teachers all pointed at George and Harold and laughed, too.

"Rats!" said Harold. "I thought we were going to have *fun* today!"

"We can still have fun," said George. "All we need is this ladder, that bag of powdered paste, and those big boxes of Styrofoam wormy thingies."

So George and Harold carried their supplies to the teachers' lounge and got down to business.

At the sink, George pulled the sprayer nozzle, while Harold carefully taped the sprayer handle in the "on" position.

Then the two boys put the nozzle back, making sure the sprayer head was pointed in the right direction.

Next, George held the ladder steady while Harold climbed up to the ceiling fan. There he began scooping generous amounts of powdered paste onto the tops of the fan blades.

"Is this right?" asked Harold.

"Yeah," said George. "Try to get most of it on the *ends* of the blades."

"Got it," said Harold.

George closed all the blinds while Harold adjusted the ceiling fan so it would turn on when the lights came on. Finally, the boys filled the refrigerator up with worm-shaped Styrofoam packaging pellets.

"This is going to be *fun*," said Harold.

"Not for the teachers!" laughed George.

CHAPTER 5
THE FUN BEGINS

An hour or so later, the buses returned to the school. All of the children got off, packed up their stuff, and got ready to go home.

Mr. Fyde, the science teacher, was on school bus duty. The rest of the teachers gathered around George and Harold and began teasing them.

"You kids sure did miss a *FUN* field trip!" said Ms. Ribble. "The pizza was *SO* delicious! Too bad *you* didn't get any!"

"I wanted to bring you back a pizza," said Mr. Meaner, "but I ate it on the bus!" He threw an empty pizza box at George and Harold's feet, and the teachers howled with laughter.

"Maybe you can lick the cheese off the box," Mr. Krupp roared.

The teachers eventually got tired of taunting George and Harold, so they retreated to the teachers' lounge to relax.

"Hey, how come it's so dark in here?" asked Mr. Meaner, as he flicked on the lights. The ceiling fan began rotating very slowly. . . .

Ms. Ribble went to the sink and turned on the faucet. Suddenly, the spray nozzle sprayed cold water all over her.

"AAAAUGH!" she screamed. "Somebody turn the water off!" The other teachers sprang up and tried to help. They all got sprayed, too.

The ceiling fan was rotating faster now, and some of the powdered paste had begun flying off the fan blades.

The teachers struggled with the faucet, pushing and shoving each other. Finally, somebody turned the water off . . . but not before everyone was thoroughly *SOAKED*!

The ceiling fan was now spinning at full speed. All of the powder on the fan blades had been flung off, and it was now floating down onto the wet teachers.

"Hey, what the—" cried Mr. Meaner.

"What's all this sticky stuff?!!?" yelled Miss Anthrope.

By now, all of the teachers were covered in gooey, sticky paste. It didn't take a genius to know that George and Harold were behind all this.

"Those brats better not have touched my diet soda!" Ms. Ribble shouted. She dashed to the refrigerator and swung the door open.

Suddenly, thousands of tiny Styrofoam pellets flew out into the room. The wind from the ceiling fan blew the pellets around and around.

Naturally, they landed on the stickiest things in the room: *the teachers*!

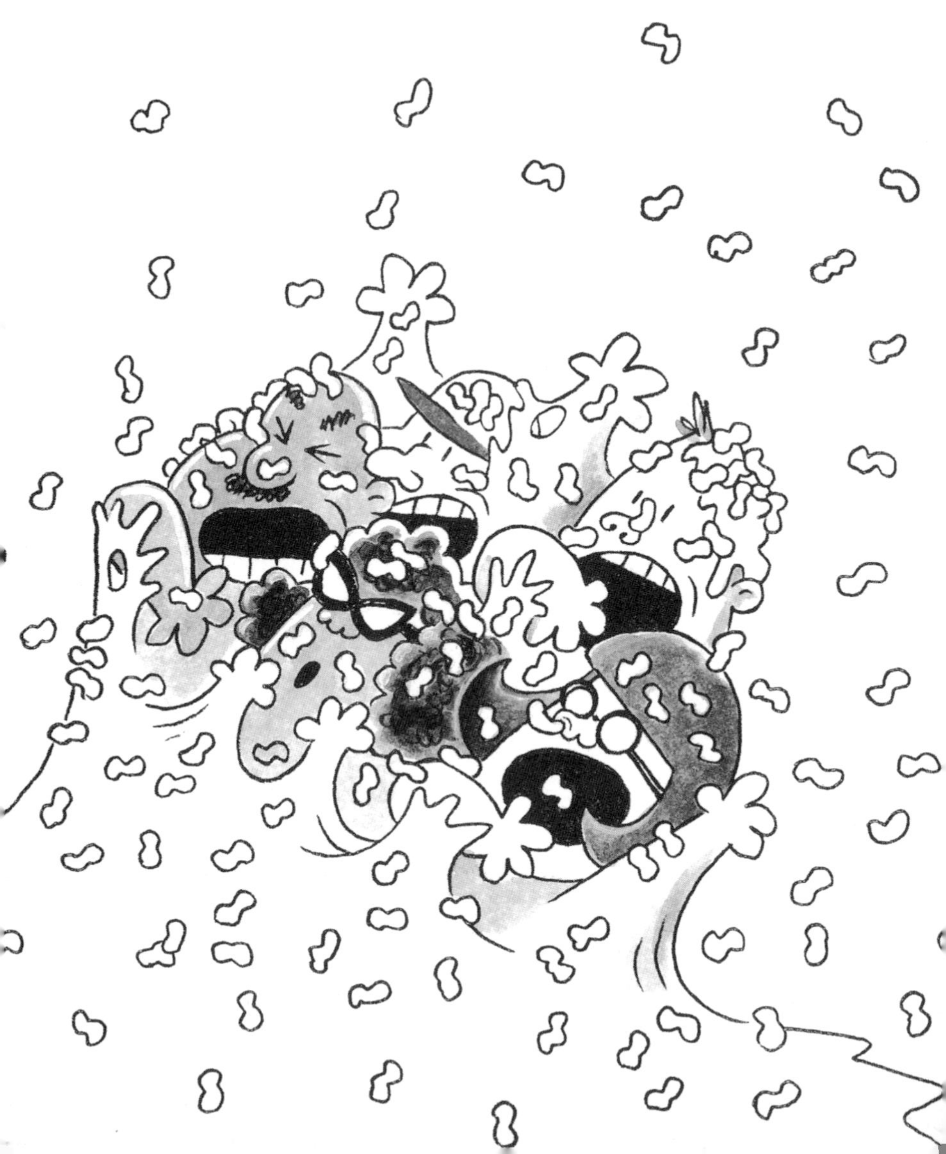

"AAAAAUUUGGGGHHHHHH!" screamed the teachers. They ran out of the teachers' lounge screaming and yelling.

George and Harold saw what looked like a group of giant evil snowmen heading straight toward them.

"I've got a good idea," said George.

"What?" asked Harold.

"*RUN!*" said George.

CHAPTER 6

BYE BYE, MR. FYDE

The next day, George and Harold's science teacher, Mr. Fyde, knocked on Mr. Krupp's door.

"What do you want?" barked Mr. Krupp.

"I've—I've come to resign," said Mr. Fyde. "I—I just can't take it anymore."

"Now hold on, bub," said Mr. Krupp. "Being a teacher is hard work! You can't just quit your job when things aren't—"

"You don't understand," said Mr. Fyde. "I think I'm cracking up!"

"What do you mean?" asked Mr. Krupp.

"Well," said Mr. Fyde. "It all started a few months ago when I had this dream that I got eaten up by a talking toilet. Then I started hearing cats and dogs meowing and growling in the classroom. Then, I imagined that the school got flooded with sticky green goop . . . and just yesterday, I thought I saw a group of abominable snowmen chasing two boys down the hallway."

"Now wait just a minute, Morty," said Mr. Krupp. "All of that can be explained."

"—And a few days ago," said Mr. Fyde, "I thought I saw a big fat bald guy in his underwear fly out the window."

"Holy *cow*!" said Mr. Krupp. "You *ARE* crazy!"

So Mr. Fyde handed in his resignation, and left Jerome Horwitz Elementary School for the greener pastures of *The Piqua Valley Home for the Reality-Challenged*.

"Now, where am I going to find a new science teacher on such short notice?" said Mr. Krupp. "Where, oh where?"

CHAPTER 7

HERE, OH HERE

Remember that Poopypants guy I was telling you about back in chapter 2? Well, things hadn't been going too well for him in the past several weeks.

Professor Poopypants had come to America to share the Shrinky-Pig 2000 and the Goosy-Grow 4000 with the world. But nobody seemed to want to hear about his inventions. They were all too busy . . .

. . . laughing at his silly name.

Poor Pippy Poopypants had been laughed out of every major scientific institution in the U.S. He'd been giggled out of Georgetown, howled out of Harvard, yuk-yukked out of Yale, snickered out of Stanford, and chuckled out of Chattanooga State Technical Community College.

Professor Poopypants was running out of money, and there was no place left for him to turn. Then, one day, the professor walked into a New York coffee shop and picked up a newspaper. And like a message from heaven, Pippy P. Poopypants found his answer.

"THAT'S IT!" he cried. "I'll become an elementary school science teacher!"

"I'll work really hard, and soon, people will come to respect me and see what a genius I am. *Then* I can introduce my great inventions to the world!"

Pippy Poopypants was certain that the one place people *wouldn't* laugh at his name was at an elementary school. "Kids are so accepting and loving," he said. "You can always count on the sweetness and innocence of children!"

CHAPTER 8

THE SWEETNESS AND INNOCENCE OF CHILDREN

"Hello, boys and girls," said the professor a week later. "I'm going to be your new science teacher. My name is . . .

. . . Professor Pippy P. Poopypants."

A-HA-HA-HA-HA-
HA-HA-HA-HA-
HA-HEE-HEE-HEE
A-HA-HA HA
HA-HA HA-HA-
HA

"Alright, settle down, boys and girls. Yes, yes, it's a funny name, I know, but let me explain how I got this name. Please, children, settle down. It's not that funny, let me assure you. Um . . . boys and girls . . . BOYS AND GIRLS! Please stop laughing! Alright, I'm going to count to ten, and when I'm done, I want all of you to quiet down so we can learn about the wonderful world of science. One, two, three, four, five, six, seven . . . eight . . . nine . . .

HA-HA-HA-HA-HA-HA-HA

. . . nine and a half . . . ummm. Children, PLEASE STOP LAUGHING! I know you're all very far behind in your lessons, and we've got a lot of catching up to do. Boys and girls! STOP IT! I'm not going to tell you again! IT'S NOT FUNNY! There's no reason at all for you to be laughing at my name! I'm sure we *all* have funny names if you think about it. STOP IT RIGHT NOW! OK, boys and girls, I'll just wait until you all settle down. I can wait. . . ."

A week later, things hadn't gotten any better. Professor Poopypants was really beginning to get angry.

"How am I going to get through to these children?" he asked himself. "Hey! I've got it! I'll create a wonderful new invention!"

CHAPTER 9

THE GERBIL JOGGER 2000

The next morning, Professor Poopypants came to school with an odd-looking miniature robot.

"Look, children," he said. "I've created a new invention using the principles of science! I call it the Gerbil Jogger 2000."

The children stopped laughing for a moment and looked with interest at Professor Poopypants's new invention.

"You see, children," said the professor, "some people like to jog, and their pets like to jog along beside them. That's fine if you have a dog or a cat, but what if you have a pet gerbil? It used to be a big problem, but not anymore!"

Professor Poopypants opened the glass dome on the Gerbil Jogger 2000 and inserted a cute, fuzzy gerbil.

The gerbil pushed his tiny legs against the simple controls, and suddenly the machine came to life. In no time at all, the gerbil was jogging around the classroom in his robot suit. The children were delighted!

"Wow!" said Connor Mancini. "Science is COOL!" All of the other children agreed.

This is wonderful! thought Professor Poopypants. *I've REACHED them! Now I can* TEACH *them!*

"Um, excuse me," said George to the professor. "What's your *middle* name?"

"My middle name," said the professor proudly, "is *Pee-Pee*. Why do you ask?"

At that point, the children picked up where they had left off: laughing at Professor Pippy *Pee-Pee* Poopypants's ridiculous name.

The professor began to shake with anger. Tiny veins in his forehead started growing, and his face turned bright red. "I can't take much more of this," the furious professor said through clenched teeth. "I think I might blow a fuse if *just one more thing* happens!"

CHAPTER 10

JUST ONE MORE THING

Soon afterward, in reading class, the children all heard the story of the Pied Piper of Hamelin.

"You know," said George, "that story gives me an idea!"

So George and Harold began working on their newest comic book: *Captain Underpants and the Pied Pooper of Piqua*.

That afternoon, they snuck into the office and ran off copies of their new adventure to sell on the playground. And everything would have been just fine if one of the third graders hadn't left his copy lying around in the hallway.

CHAPTER 11
CAPTAIN UNDERPANTS AND THE PIED POOPER OF PIQUA
PP
PP
PP
PP
By GeorGe BeArd and Harold Hutchins

CAPTAIN UNDERPANTS
And The PIED POOPER of PIQUA

Story By George Beard • Pictures by Harold Hutchins

Onse upon a time in the city of PIQUA, OHIO, there was A sciense Teacher whose name was Pippy PoopyPants

my middel name is Pee-Pee.

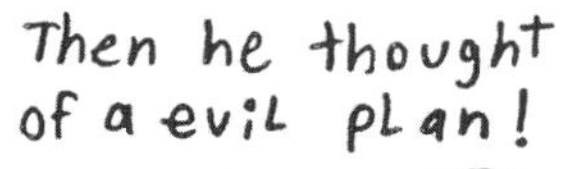

Soon, Professor Poopypantses Army of Girbel Jogger Two Thousends were off on a evil RAMPAGE.

Professer Poopypants and his evil Army Rounded up ALL The children.
Follow me! HA HAHA

This Looks Like A JOB for...

CAPTAin UNDERPAnTS!

what seems to Be the problem?
I'm Taking These kids To be my SLAves

And just who Do you Think You Are?
I'm Professer POOPYPAnts

HA HA HA HA HA HA HA HA HA
HA HA HA HA HA
HA HA HA
HA HA HA HA HA

Professor Poopypants WAS really mad. So He pressed A BUTTON on his bowtie...

..MORE POWERFUL Than Boxer Shorts...
OWIE!

...And Abel To Leap taLL buildings without Getting A Wedgie!
TRA-LA-LAAA!

Professor Poopypants chased our Hero To A AUTO JUNKYArd.

I've GoT you Now, WAISTband WArrior!
KLUNK

Now I'm Gunna Crush You!
OFF
START
BiG CRUSHer Thingy 2000

CAPTAin Underpants Pressed a button on his "UTILITY WAIStband."
CLICK!

And out popped the Tiny Toilet of Truth.
CLICK

CAPTAin Underpants Aimed The Tiny Toilet of Truth AT Robo-Pippy.
BCT2

FLUSH!

I'm Rusted!

CAPTAIN UNDERPANTS SAVED THE DAY!
BUT WHAT ABOUT THE EVIL GIRBLES?
They're not evil!
PP
PP

Look! Professor Poopypants was controling them with this!!!

IS IT MUSIC?
no.
CHER'S Greatest HITS
Listen...

BABE, I GOT YOU BABE...
AAAAH
Please, God make it stop!
Help!
This would make anybody turn evil.

So Captain Underpants destroyed the controller.
TRA-LA-LAAA
HALLY-LOOYA!
CRUNCH

HOORAY for CAPTAIN UNDERPANTS!
PP
PP
PP
THE END

NOTISE: ALL ANIMAL cruelty WAS simulated. No Actual Girbles were Forsed To listen to CHer.

Treehouse Comix

CHAPTER 12

PROFESSOR P. GOES CRA-Z

In his entire life, Professor Poopypants had never been as angry as he was at that very moment. As he stood in the hallway, something inside his fragile brain snapped. He began shaking and sweating uncontrollably.

Suddenly, a wicked smile stretched across the professor's face. He staggered toward his empty classroom, mumbling to himself and giggling. He had hit rock bottom, and he decided to pull the rest of the planet down with him. Pippy P. Poopypants was going to take over the world!

But before I can tell you that story, I have to tell you . . . oh, never mind. I'll just tell you that story.

CHAPTER 13

HONEY, I SHRUNK THE SCHOOL

Professor Poopypants opened the storage closet in his classroom and took out the Shrinky-Pig 2000 and the Goosy-Grow 4000. He also grabbed the empty Gerbil Jogger 2000, and stumbled outside with his inventions.

The crazed professor giggled wildly to himself as he aimed the Goosy-Grow 4000 at the Gerbil Jogger 2000.

"GGGGLLUUZZZZZZZZRRRRRT!"

Suddenly, the Gerbil Jogger 2000 grew ten stories high.

Professor Poopypants began his long climb up the side of the giant Gerbil Jogger 2000. It took almost an hour, but eventually he reached the huge glass dome at the top and squeezed his way inside.

"Mommy?" said a little boy who was walking by with his mother. "A little old man just crawled into a giant robot suit and is about to take over a school!"

"Oh, for heaven's sake!" said his mother. "Where do you come up with this nonsense?!!? Next you'll be telling me that a giant man in his underwear is fighting the huge robot in the middle of the city!"

Professor Poopypants was now in control of the colossal Gerbil Jogger 2000. He reached down with its mighty arm, picked up the Shrinky-Pig 2000, and aimed it at the school.

"BLLLLLLZZZZRRRRK!"

Just then, George and Harold looked out the window. "Hey," said George, "isn't that the gerbil robot thingy?"

"Yeah," said Harold. "Why is it so big?"

"I don't know," said George, "but it's getting bigger by the second!"

"Um . . . ," said Harold, "I don't think it's getting bigger . . . I think *WE'RE* getting *smaller*!"

CHAPTER 14

THE PERILOUS PLOT

Professor Poopypants reached down and picked up the tiny school with his giant robotic hand. Everyone screamed in horror.

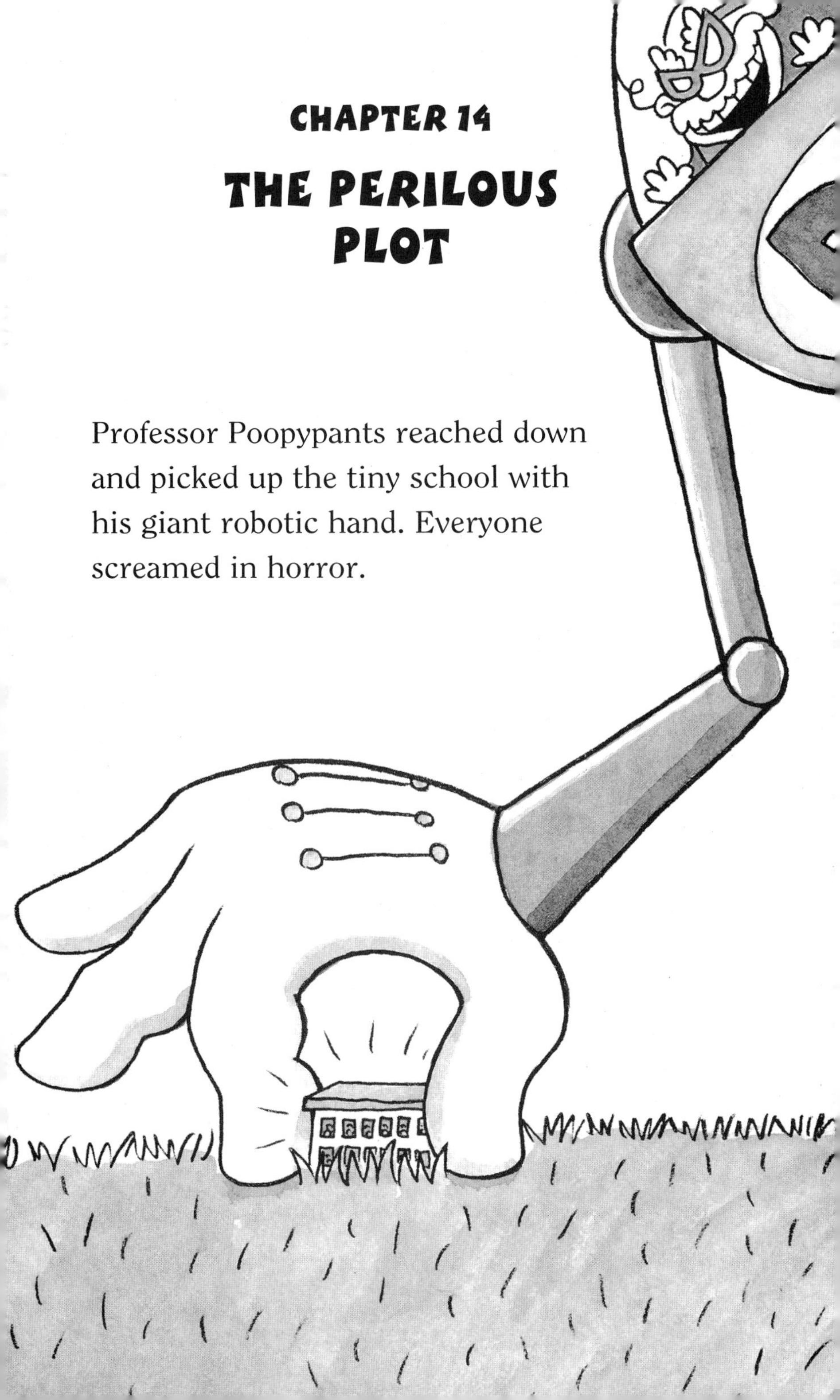

In no time at all, Eyewitness Newswoman Ingrid Ashley was on the scene.

"What do you want from us?" shouted reporter Ashley.

"I want . . . a *pencil*!" screamed Professor Poopypants.

"A pencil?!!?" asked Reporter Ashley. "Here—take mine." She tossed a yellow #2 pencil toward the giant robot.

Professor Poopypants reached down with his giant robot arm, picked up the Goosy-Grow 4000, and aimed it at the pencil.

"GGGGLLUUZZZZZZZZRRRRRT!"

The pencil grew to the size of a tree trunk, and Professor Poopypants grabbed it.

"Follow me," he said.

The giant robot led the news crew to the center of downtown Piqua. There, he found three large white billboards. He put down the Shrinky-Pig 2000 and the Goosy-Grow 4000, and began writing on the billboards with his giant pencil.

CHAPTER 15
THE NAME CHANGE-O-CHART 2000

Professor Poopypants spent several minutes jotting down a complex code on the three giant billboards.

George and Harold, along with nearly a thousand of their fellow shrunken students, watched the mad professor from the terrifying clutch of his giant robotic hand.

"What is that crazy guy up to?" asked Mr. Krupp from his office window.

"I'LL TELL YOU," shouted Pippy Poopypants. "Everybody on the planet must now change their normal names into silly names using these three charts! Anyone who refuses will get *SHRUNK*!"

"How do the charts work?" asked Mr. Krupp.

"It's easy," said Professor Poopypants. "What's your first name?"

"Er . . . , I'm not telling," said Mr. Krupp.

"WHAT IS YOUR FIRST NAME?!!?" shouted Professor Poopypants.

"Alright, alright," said Mr. Krupp. "It's, uh . . . *Benny*." All of the children giggled.

"So the first letter of your first name is *B*," said Pippy. "Now look at the first chart and find the letter *B*."

Mr. Krupp looked at the chart. "It says 'B = Lumpy,'" he whined.

"Good!" said Professor Poopypants. "Your NEW first name is '*LUMPY*!'"

All of the children laughed.

"*Lumpy* Krupp?!!?" moaned Mr. Krupp. "I don't want to be called 'Lumpy Krupp.'"

"You won't!" laughed Professor Poopypants. "Because you have to change your *last* name, too!"

"Uh-oh," said Mr. Krupp.

"Your last name is 'Krupp,'" said the professor, "which starts with a *K* and ends with a *P*. Now find the letter *K* on the second chart, and the letter *P* on the third chart."

Mr. Krupp looked at the two charts.

"It says, 'K = Potty' and 'P = biscuits.'"

"Wonderful!" shouted the professor. "Your new last name is 'Pottybiscuits.'"

"Oh, no!" groaned the principal. "My new name is '*Lumpy Pottybiscuits*!'"

The children all howled with laughter.

"Don't laugh *too* hard, kiddies," said Professor Poopypants. "You all have to change your names, too, or I'll shrink you again!"

Well, as you can imagine, nobody wanted to get shrunk *twice*! So everybody looked at the three charts and figured out their new, silly names.

Stephanie Yarkoff became "Snotty Gorillabreath." Robbie Staenberg became "Loopy Pizzapants," and poor little Janet Warwick became "Poopsie Chucklebutt."

"This may be the most horrible moment in all of human history," said the local news reporter to her audience. "It seems that everyone on Earth must now change his or her name to avoid getting shrunk! Good luck to you all!

"This is Chim-Chim Diaperbrains reporting for Eyewitness News. Now, back to you, Booger."

CHAPTER 16

FLUFFY AND CHEESEBALL

This is Fluffy Toiletnose and Cheeseball Wafflefanny. Fluffy is the kid on the left with the tie and the flat-top. Cheeseball is the one on the right with the T-shirt and the bad haircut. Remember that now.

"We've got to do something," cried Fluffy.

"But what?" said Cheeseball. "We're smaller than two mice . . . what could we possibly do?"

"Let's go find our old friend, Captain Underpants!" said Fluffy.

So Fluffy and Cheeseball ran to Mr. Pottybiscuits's office and found him cowering under his desk.

"I can't believe I'm about to do this," said Fluffy, "but here goes nothing!"

Fluffy snapped his fingers.

SNAP!

Suddenly, a strange change came over Lumpy Pottybiscuits. His worried frown quickly turned into a heroic smile. He rose from behind his desk and thrust out his chest.

In no time at all, Mr. Pottybiscuits had removed his outer clothing and tied a red curtain around his neck.

"Tra-La-LAAAA!" sang the hero. "Captain Underpants is here!"

"Cool!" said Cheeseball. "But from now on you have to call yourself 'Buttercup Chickenfanny.' The guy in the gerbil suit says so!"

"Hey," said Captain Underpants, "I don't take orders from *ANYBODY*!"

"Great," said Fluffy. "Now fly out that window and bring back that big machine thingy with the Lava Lamp on top."

"Yes, *SIR*," said Captain Underpants.

CHAPTER 17

CAPTAIN UNDERPANTS TO THE RESCUE

Captain Underpants flew down to the ground and grabbed the Goosy-Grow 4000. But on his way back up, he was spotted by Professor Poopypants.

The evil professor zapped Captain Underpants with a bolt of energy from the Shrinky-Pig 2000.

"BLLLLLLZZZZRRRRK!"

Suddenly, the Waistband Warrior began to shrink even *smaller* than before. He flew back to the tiny school carrying an extremely small Goosy-Grow 4000, and he dropped it into Fluffy's hand.

"Hey, where's Captain Underpants?" asked Fluffy.

"I don't know," said Cheeseball. "I think he got shrunk so small that we can't see him anymore."

"Well," said Fluffy, "at least we have this little invention thingy."

"How's that going to help us?" asked Cheeseball.

"I saw Professor Poopypants use it to make that pencil grow really big," said Fluffy. "It's our only hope of ever getting back to normal size!"

"I hope it still works," said Cheeseball.

Fluffy and Cheeseball dashed to the school kitchen and climbed up the ladder onto the roof.

"Maybe if we zap the school with this thing, everybody will grow back to normal size," said Fluffy.

"Good idea," said Cheeseball. "Then we can all run away!"

CHAPTER 18

ARE YOU THERE, GOD? IT'S US, FLUFFY AND CHEESEBALL

Fluffy pointed the Goosy-Grow 4000 at the roof of the school and got ready to press the button. But the boys were spotted by Professor Poopypants. Quickly, he turned his mighty robotic hand, and Fluffy and Cheeseball slid off the roof. Downward they tumbled through the air.

"Oh, NO," shouted Cheeseball. "We're DOOMED!"

"Wait a second," cried Fluffy. "Do you have a piece of paper on you?"

"Yeah," screamed Cheeseball. "Right here in my pocket. But what good is it gonna do us now?"

"Quick!" cried Fluffy. "Fold it into a paper airplane!"

"What *kind* of paper airplane?" asked Cheeseball.

"ANY KIND!" screamed Fluffy. "JUST DO IT NOW!"

Quickly, Cheeseball folded the paper into a goofy-looking glider. “How’s this?” he screamed.

“Great!” yelled Fluffy. “Now hold it steady!” Fluffy pointed the tiny Goosy-Grow 4000 at Cheeseball’s airplane, and he pressed the button.

“GGGGLLUUZZZZZZZZRRRRRT!”

Suddenly, Cheeseball's airplane grew to an enormous size. Fluffy and Cheeseball flopped down into it, and the paper airplane took off, gliding through the air.

"Oh, MAN!" cried Cheeseball. "I can't believe that worked!"

"We're not out of this yet!" yelled Fluffy.

CHAPTER 19
THE FLIGHT OF THE GOOFY GLIDER

Fluffy and Cheeseball had to admit that it was pretty cool flying over the city streets on a paper airplane. They didn't even seem to mind the fact that they were only about an inch tall each.

But you can probably imagine the boys' concern when they started heading straight for a wood chipper.

“Oh, NO!” cried Fluffy. “We’re gonna get, um . . . *WOOD CHIPPERED* to death!”

Cheeseball couldn’t look. He put his hands over his eyes and waited for the inevitable.

But suddenly, *SWOOOOSH!* The paper airplane swerved sharply and missed the wood chipper altogether.

“Hey!” cried Fluffy. “How did that happen?”

“I don’t know,” said Cheeseball. “*I’m* not steering this thing!”

The boys had barely caught their breath when a small dog noticed the airplane and came running after them.

"Oh, NO!" cried Cheeseball. "We're gonna get eaten by a *WIENER DOG*!"

Fluffy covered *his* eyes this time.

But wouldn't you know it, the airplane swerved sharply upward and out of the range of the little dog altogether.

"Are you doing that?" asked Cheeseball.

"No," said Fluffy. "It must be the wind!"

Finally, the paper airplane landed in a wet, sticky pile of hot blacktop.

"Yuck!" said Fluffy. "What could be worse than gettin' stuck in a pile of *blacktop*?"

"Maybe getting crushed by a big steamroller thingy," said Cheeseball.

"You sure have an active imagination," said Fluffy.

"No, I don't," said Cheeseball, as he pointed upward. *"Look!"*

"Oh, NO!" screamed Fluffy. "We're gonna get *STEAMROLLER THINGIED* to death!"

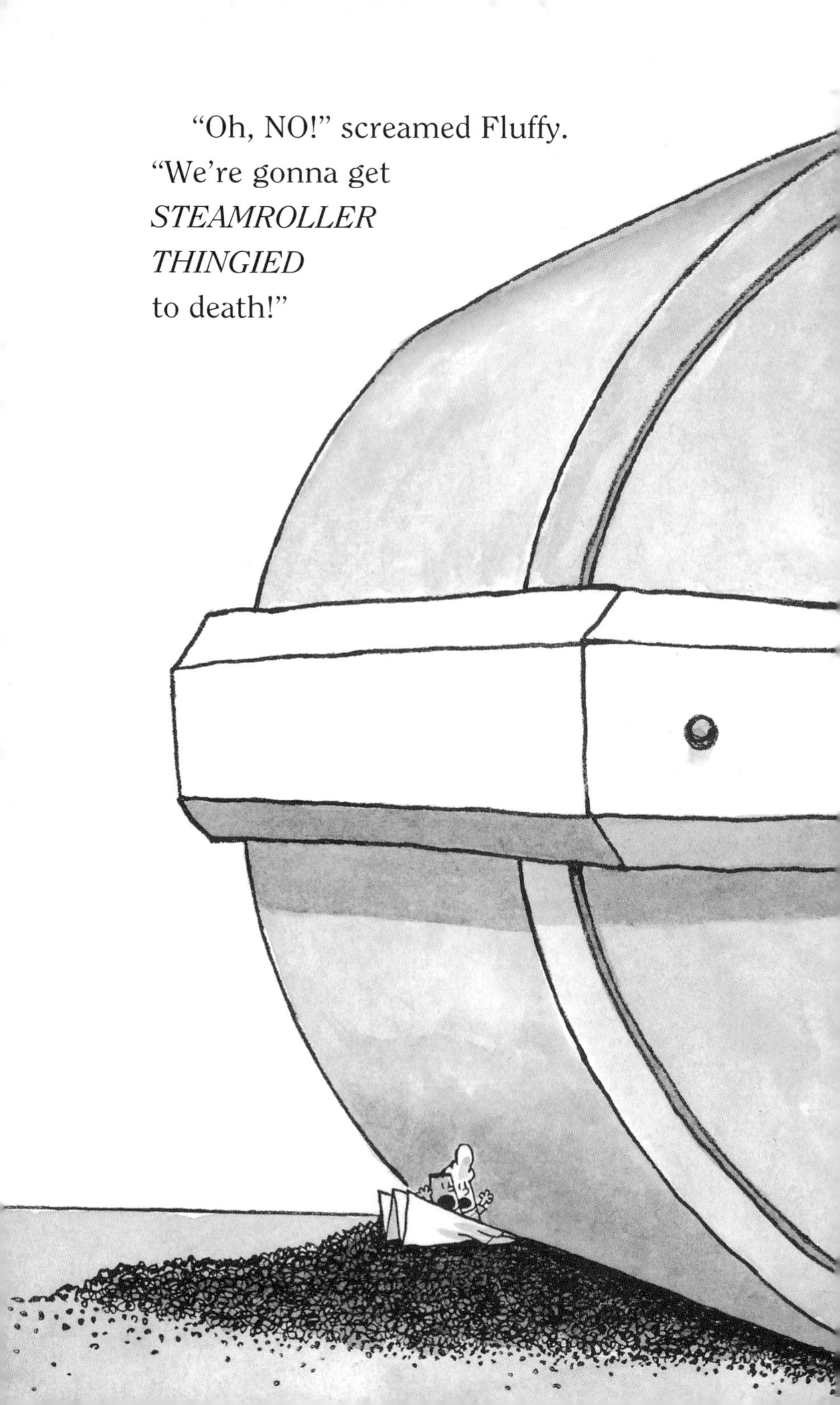

Just then, the boys were yanked up by the backs of their shirts and carried off through the air to safety.

"Something's got a hold of us!" cried Cheeseball. "But I can't see what it is!"

"It must be Captain Underpants," said Fluffy. "We just can't see him because he's so small!"

"Hey," said Cheeseball, "I'll bet he was steering the airplane out of danger, too!"

"*OUR HERO!*" the boys shouted.

CHAPTER 20

X-TRA, X-TRA, X-TRA, X-TRA, X-TRA, X-TRA, X-TRA, X-TRA, X-TRA LARGE UNDERPANTS

Fluffy and Cheeseball landed safely in an abandoned alley.

"We've got to enlarge Captain Underpants so he can fight Professor Poopypants," said Fluffy. "The fate of the entire planet is in our hands!"

"But how can we enlarge him if we can't even see him?" asked Cheeseball.

"Good question," said Fluffy.

"Wait," said Cheeseball. "I've got an idea." He called out as loud as he could: "Captain Underpants! We can't see you, but if you can hear us, fly over and land on my finger. We have a machine that can make you big again."

The boys waited a few seconds.

"Look, Fluffy!" said Cheeseball. "There he is! See? He's that little tiny speck on my finger. Now just aim the machine at that little speck . . . but don't zap my finger, OK?"

"Don't worry," said Fluffy. "I'm a great shot with this thing. I won't zap your . . .

"GGGGLLUUZZZZZZZZRRRRRT!"

. . . OOPS! Sorry."

The good news was that Captain Underpants had grown larger and was now visible. The bad news was, well, let's just say that Cheeseball was going to have an awful hard time picking his nose with his right hand from now on.

Fluffy gave Captain Underpants a few more shots from the Goosy-Grow 4000. The Waistband Warrior grew and grew and grew until he was ten stories high.

Finally, the colossal captain headed toward the preposterous professor. A showdown was about to begin.

The little boy from chapter 13 happened to be walking by with his mother again. He looked up and saw a giant man in his underwear getting ready to fight a huge robot in the middle of the city.

"Mommy?" said the little boy.

"What?" asked his mother.

"Umm . . . never mind," said the boy.

CHAPTER 21

THE INCREDIBLY GRAPHIC VIOLENCE CHAPTER (IN FLIP-O-RAMA™)

WARNING:

The following chapter contains scenes that are so intense and horrific, they may not be suitable for viewing by people who can't take a joke.

If you are easily offended, or if you tend to blame all of society's evils on TV shows and cartoon characters, please run to your nearest supermarket and get a life. They're located in the "Get Real" section next to the clues.

Good luck!

Introducing
FLIP-
Throughout the history of great art, there have been many times when artists have defined their own unique styles, creating what is known as a "movement." For example, there was the "Renaissance Movement," the "Impressionist Movement," and even the "Pop Art Movement."
Today, many art scholars agree that the early 21st century may go down in history as the "Flip-O-Rama Movement." Let's enjoy this great art form, and marvel at its emerging cultural significance, shall we?

HERE'S HOW IT WORKS!

STEP 1

Place your *left* hand inside the dotted lines marked "LEFT HAND HERE." Hold the book open *flat*.

STEP 2

Grasp the *right-hand* page with your right thumb and index finger (inside the dotted lines marked "RIGHT THUMB HERE").

STEP 3

Now *quickly* flip the right-hand page back and forth until the picture appears to be *animated*.

(For extra fun, try adding your own sound-effects!)

FLIP-O-RAMA 1

(pages 123 and 125)

Remember, flip *only* page 123.
While you are flipping, be sure you
can see the picture on page 123
and the one on page 125.
If you flip quickly, the two
pictures will start to look like
one *animated* picture.

Don't forget to
add your own sound-effects!

LEFT HAND HERE

PROFESSOR POOPYPANTS PACKED A POWERFUL PUNCH!

RIGHT THUMB HERE

RIGHT
INDEX
FINGER
HERE

PROFESSOR POOPYPANTS PACKED A POWERFUL PUNCH!

FLIP-O-RAMA 2

(pages 127 and 129)

Remember, flip *only* page 127.
While you are flipping, be sure you
can see the picture on page 127
and the one on page 129.
If you flip quickly, the two
pictures will start to look like
one *animated* picture.

Don't forget to
add your own sound-effects!

LEFT HAND HERE

BUT THE HEAD-BUTTIN' HERO HALTED THE HORROR!

RIGHT THUMB HERE

RIGHT
INDEX
FINGER
HERE

BUT THE HEAD-BUTTIN' HERO HALTED THE HORROR!

FLIP-O-RAMA 3

(pages 131 and 133)

Remember, flip *only* page 131.
While you are flipping, be sure you
can see the picture on page 131
and the one on page 133.
If you flip quickly, the two
pictures will start to look like
one *animated* picture.

Don't forget to
add your own sound-effects!

LEFT HAND HERE

THE BRIEF-WEARIN' BANDIT BATTLED THE BIONIC BEHEMOTH!

RIGHT THUMB HERE

RIGHT
INDEX
FINGER
HERE

THE BRIEF-WEARIN' BANDIT BATTLED THE BIONIC BEHEMOTH!

FLIP-O-RAMA 4

(pages 135 and 137)

Remember, flip *only* page 135.
While you are flipping, be sure you
can see the picture on page 135
and the one on page 137.
If you flip quickly, the two
pictures will start to look like
one *animated* picture.

Don't forget to
add your own sound-effects!

LEFT HAND HERE

THE WAISTBAND WARRIOR WON THE WAR!

RIGHT
INDEX
FINGER
HERE

THE WAISTBAND WARRIOR WON THE WAR!

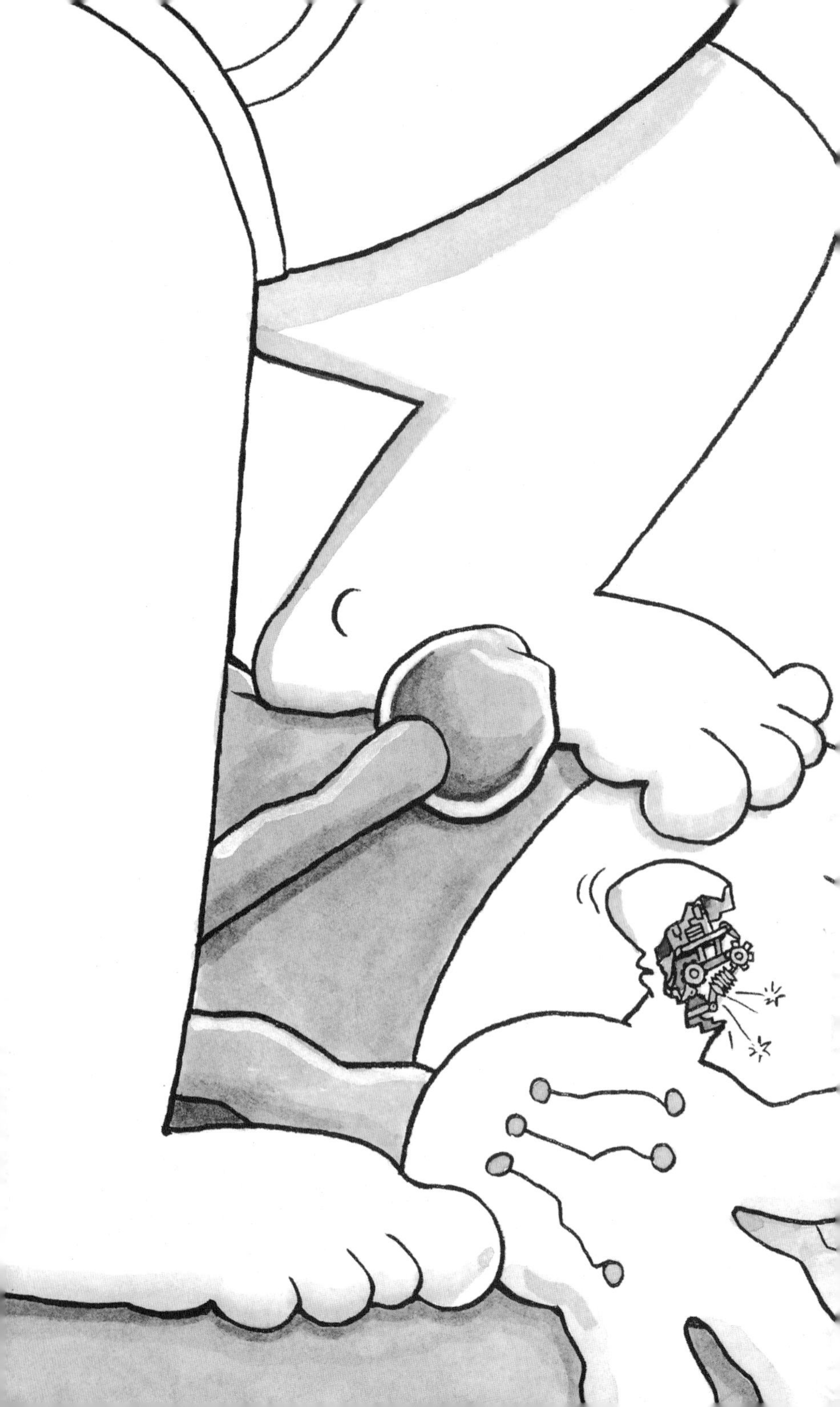

CHAPTER 22
THE TWENTY-SECOND CHAPTER

Professor Poopypants had been defeated, and everybody in the school cheered wildly. They were still small, but at least they got their old names back.

"I'm sure glad I don't have a silly name anymore," said Ms. Ribble.

"Me, too," said Mr. Rected.

"Hooray!" cried George. "Let's all give Captain Underpants a big *hand*!"

Harold was not amused.

"Oops . . . ," said George. "Sorry."

"That's OK," said Harold. "Just gimme that invention thing so I can zap us back to normal!"

Harold held the Goosy-Grow 4000 in his giant hand and zapped George and himself (that is, every part of himself *EXCEPT* his giant hand).

"GGGGLLUUZZZZZZZZRRRRRT!"

Suddenly, George and Harold were back to their normal sizes again.

"Boy," said George, "we sure have tested the limits of science today!"

"Yep!" said Harold, "*and* the limits of our readers' willing suspension of disbelief!"

"Er . . . *yyyeah,*" said George, "that, too!"

George and Harold picked up their tiny school and carried it back to where it belonged. George got ready to zap the school with the Goosy-Grow 4000, while Harold prepared to zap Captain Underpants with the Shrinky-Pig 2000.

"I sure hope this works," said George.

"Me, too," said Harold.

CHAPTER 23

TO MAKE A LONG STORY SHORT

It did.

CHAPTER 24
THE CHAPTER BEFORE THE LAST CHAPTER

George took Captain Underpants over to the bushes behind the school and ordered him to dress back up like Mr. Krupp.

"Let's go, bub," said George. "We haven't got all day!"

Then Harold had some fun with the garden hose. In no time at all, Mr. Krupp was back to his old nasty self again.

Soon the cops showed up to arrest Professor Poopypants.

"There's one thing I don't understand," said George to the professor. "Wouldn't it have been *smarter* to change *your own name* instead of forcing the rest of the world to change theirs?"

"Gosh," said Professor Poopypants, "I never thought of that!"

A few weeks later, George and Harold received a letter from the Piqua State Penitentiary.

Dear George and Harold,

Sorry about trying to overthrow the world and everything. I've decided to take your advice and change my name so that people won't laugh at me any-more.

From now on I'll be going by my Grandfather's name (on my mother's side). It's such a relief knowing that nobody will ever make fun of my name again.

Signed,
Tippy Tinkletrousers

HA HA
HA HA-HA-
HAW
HEE-
HA
HA
HA
HA
HA
PIQU
STAT
PEN

CHAPTER 25

THE CHAPTER AFTER THE CHAPTER BEFORE THE LAST CHAPTER

"You know," said George, "I really learned something today."

"What's that?" asked Harold.

"I learned that it's not nice to make fun of people," said George.

"Wow," said Harold. "I think this is the first time one of our stories ever had a *moral*!"

"Probably the last time, too," said George.

"Let's hope so," said Harold.

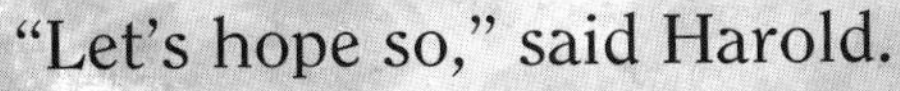

But George and Harold had forgotten all about the *other* moral they had learned along the way, which was: "Don't ever, ever, *EVER* hypnotize your principal."

Because if you do, your life can go from bad to worse . . .

. . . at the *snap* of a finger!

"OH, NO!" screamed Harold.

"HERE WE GO AGAIN!" screamed George.

TRA-LA LAAAAA

If you feel you have suffered great emotional distress from having your name changed by Professor Poopypants, please visit

www.scholastic.com/captainunderpants/funstuff

to download something fun!

...WATCH YOUR BACK!!!

ABOUT THE AUTHOR

When Dav Pilkey was a kid, he suffered from ADHD, dyslexia, and behavioral problems. Dav was so disruptive in class that his teachers made him sit out in the hall every day. Fortunately, Dav loved to draw and make up stories. He spent his time in the hallway creating his own original comic books.

In the second grade, Dav Pilkey created a comic book about a superhero named Captain Underpants. His teacher ripped it up and told him he couldn't spend the rest of his life making silly books.

Fortunately, Dav was not a very good listener.